It's Never Too Late

It's Never Too Late

JON LEWIS

It's Never Too Late

Copyright © 2023 by Jon Lewis. All rights reserved.

No part of this publication may be reproduced, stored in a retrieval system or transmitted in any way by any means, electronic, mechanical, photocopy, recording or otherwise without the prior permission of the author except as provided by USA copyright law.

The opinions expressed by the author are not necessarily those of URLink Print and Media.

1603 Capitol Ave., Suite 310 Cheyenne, Wyoming USA 82001
1-888-980-6523 | admin@urlinkpublishing.com

URLink Print and Media is committed to excellence in the publishing industry.

Book design copyright © 2023 by URLink Print and Media. All rights reserved.

Published in the United States of America

ISBN 978-1-68486-687-8 (Paperback)
ISBN 978-1-68486-688-5 (Digital)

19.12.2023

Contents

Preface 7
Who are the players? 9
Meeting 11
Sleep Over 13
The Club 15
First Road Trip 17
Second Road Trip 19
Family 21
Family Golf 23
Breakup 25
Getting Back 27
Still Going 29
Author's Bio 31

Preface

What is love between a man and a woman? I suspect each of us has a different view of this. Some think it can only happen between young people. Others believe it can happen at any age.

What determines if it is really love? How do they get along together? Do they have similar activities that they participate in? What about politics? Can they differ and still love each other?

You will see many references to golf. They both loved the game and participated in it often. However, as time passes you will notice that it is not the underlying aspect of the relationship.

You will see that both of them are of good heart and love people. Although they differ in their politics it had no deduction from their love for each other.

Who are the players?

He is Dick and she is Jane. Dick lost his wife about 15 years ago. Jane lost her husband about 10 years ago. Dick's wife passed suddenly from a drug overdose. Jane lost her husband after several years of bad health. She nursed him for several years before he passed.

Both are retired and living alone in cities 30 miles from each other. Both were tired of living alone and being by themselves. Dick had started dating over the internet several years ago but never found a lady with more than being friendly. Jane started dating over the internet also.

Both loved golf. Dick was better than average but Jane was not very good but loved the game anyway. Dick had been trained by Bruce Simms and Susan Johnson. He studied the game and understood the good and bad ways of playing.

Jane could not hit her irons. However, Dick was patient and worked with her to improve. As time passed she got better and better and finally could use her irons in the game

Golf had a big influence on the two of them getting closer and closer. It's one thing to sit together watching TV or doing something else but to team up in a specific activity is even better.

Meeting

Their first meeting was at Jane's house. They carried on a conversation on several topics. At time passed they started to like each other. Then they kissed. Wow! It was starting to get interesting.

Sleep Over

As time passed and the relationship improved they decided that Dick should spend the night at Jane's. It worked very well. The romance grew fast. This was usually on a Saturday night.

On Sunday mornings Jane went to mass. Dick joined her a few times but usually stayed at Jane's house. He would read parts of the newspaper and watch TV.

When Jane returned from mass she fixed breakfast for both of them. They both read different parts of the newspaper and watched TV. It was a time that both enjoyed immensely. It would become a special activity for both of them forever. This will be mentioned later as time passed.

As time passed the sleep over became part of the relationship. Dick started bringing some of his clothes and putting them in the closet. This way he could dress for any occasion. It would work out well as time passed.

The Club

Jane belonged to a club. Once a week she would meet her friends there. All were married so there were both men and women at the meetings. All were drinking mixed drinks, wine, or beer. The women sat at one end of the big table and men at the other end. Jane Introduced Dick to all of them.

Jane got involved in conversations with the other ladies. Dick started conversation with the guys. The guys accepted Dick and they got along just fine. Some even gave Dick some bullets for his gun so he could shoot some of the wild game on his property.

This became a regular routine for Dick and Jane. They both enjoyed it.

Some Saturdays the club had a special occasion with a band and dancing. Dick and Jane sometimes attended this event. Just like the weekday events they all sat at a big table together. Mostly the same folks that got together at the weekday events. Sometimes a new person joined them. Some danced but most of the time was spent in conversations. All enjoyed the time together.

First Road Trip

Jane had a program where she got special benefits when traveling away from home. One time they decided to go to Arizona for a trip. They could stay at a hotel and play golf together. It was a great hotel with lovely rooms and great view. They got to spend time in the swimming pool and hot tub. It was great relaxation for both. Time spent time together in a different atmosphere.

They also got to play golf at a great course. They didn't play any better but the view was wonderful. After golf they had lunch at the course club. Then back to the hotel for more relaxation.

The trip was a long one. Jane drove her car because she knew where she was going and how to get there. Because of the distance they stayed in a hotel on the way there. They had one stop for gas and relaxation on the way back. It was a great way to enjoy each other in a different atmosphere.

Second Road Trip

They enjoyed the first road trip so much they decided to take another road trip. This time it was to the beaches on the Gulf of Mexico in Texas. The distance was not as far as the first road trip so there were no stops to and from the beach. They stayed in a place next to the beach.

Not far from the beach was a golf course. As you can imagine they went to play golf on the course. It was difficult getting there but they made it. Both played well and enjoyed every minute. The course was in good shape and the view was wonderful.

The beach was close to where they were staying. Both got to get in the water and avoid the waves. They didn't spend enough time when they went to the beach so neither got sunburn. They got to enjoy some romance when both were ready.

Just another good time spent with two friends that were also lovers. It seems like each day the two of them became closer and closer. True love is so good for the soul.

Family

One time Dick's family came to see him on a weekend. Jane came to Dick's and met Dick's family. It was Dick's kids and grandkids. All the kids and grandkids loved Jane. Likewise, Jane loved all of them. It was an introduction to another part of Dick's life new to his family.

This showed how huge Jane's heart was. She was filled with love and Dick recognized it. It was one more aspect of the relationship growing stronger.

Family Golf

Dick had 3 kids that also knew how to play golf. He had one son and two daughters. One weekend they came to Jane's house where Dick was there. All five of them went to the golf course. After some discussion they decided to play a scramble. That's where each player on the team shoots and the team decides to play the best shot for all of them to play the next shot until the hole is finished.

They decided that the three girls would be on one team and the two boys on the other team. Don't remember which team won but it was so much fun for all of us.

It was such a wonderful time. It was two lovers and kids of one all together. There were lots of smiles and laughter. All enjoyed the time and togetherness. All hoped for a repeat in the future.

Breakup

Dick was a smoker. One day it was found that he had lung cancer. Jane took him for treatment which was successful. Dick quit smoking for four months.

Dick played golf twice a week with the old guys at his course. One day they brought a guest who smoked. Dick borrowed a cig from the guest. Next thing Dick was smoking again.

When Jane discovered that Dick was smoking again, she thought it was over. Her husband got sick and she nursed him for years before he passed. She did not want to do that again with Dick. It was too painful for her with nursing her husband. It would be more painful with Dick.

As such, she kicked Dick out. She helped him get his clothes and belongings to his car. Was it all over between them? Time will tell.

Getting Back

There was so much love between Dick and Jane it was terrible for both of them to not see each other again. It came to the point that they started emailing each other and talking on the phone. As time passed they decided to try their old process of breakfast at Jane's on Sunday mornings.

First time they did this it was difficult for both of them. However, their love for each other forced them to get together and see how it goes. There was no romance when it first started and no kissing or hugging. It was just being there in presence of each other that made it good for both of them.

Still Going

As time passed and them seeing each other on Sunday mornings, things improved. There was no hugging but just a brother/sister kiss on arrival. Both enjoyed breakfast and time together.

With the two of them in love with each other the love will last forever. At least until one is in a grave and maybe even longer.

This is the kind of love most people only dream about. It is the joining of two loving people always thinking of others. It's almost beyond imagination.

This kind of love will never end.

Author's Bio

Jon Lewis is an independent thinker. He likes to hear all sides of a situation before making up his own mind. He likes to apply science and history to all situations. He is surprised that he is alone here. He has attended meetings of the Democrat Party, Republican Party, and Tea Party. He enjoyed them all.

He has an advanced degree in physics and has had two careers. First was as an engineer and second as owner of a business in the health insurance area. He has one copyright in computer software. When working as an engineer he worked part time in real estate and life insurance.

Can I Help You was his first book. All who read it loved it. Some couldn't put it down until finished.

Help Save America is his second book. Again all who read it loved it.

Want A Good Retirement is his third book. Just published so no reviews yet

Child Guidance has started but will be awhile before published.

www.ingramcontent.com/pod-product-compliance
Lightning Source LLC
LaVergne TN
LVHW021745060526
838200LV00052B/3475